North Star

By Jenny Oldfield

Illustrated by Gillian Martin

First published in Great Britain in 2006
by Hodder Children's Books

1

A Catalogue record for this book is available from the British Library

ISBN-10: 0 340 91841 1
ISBN-13: 9780340918418

Printed and bound in Great Britain by
Bookmarque Ltd, Croydon, Surrey

The paper and board used in this paperback by Hodder Children's Books are natural recyclable products made from wood grown in sustainable forests. The manufacturing processes conform to the environmental regulations of the country of origin.

Hodder Children's Books
A division of Hodder Headline Limited
338 Euston Road, London NW1 3BH

Chapter One

"Let me out of here!" Krista muttered. She was in town on a cold December morning, buying presents for her friends, Janey, Alice and Carrie.

Crowds of anxious shoppers elbowed each other out of the way.

"Watch where you're going!" an old lady cried, barging into Krista with her shopping bags.

A man on a bike mounted the pavement and whizzed across her path. A crowd of kids blocked her way.

"Yeah, give me ponies and stables any day!" Krista sighed. She stopped in a doorway to peer inside her plastic bag and check the presents she'd managed to buy so far – hair accessory for Alice, sparkly address book for Janey, photo frame for Carrie. *Enough for today,* she thought. *Now at last I can get out of this place!*

"Hey, Krista!" a voice said from across the busy street, and Alice Henderson made her way towards her.

Quickly Krista closed up her plastic bag, wondering if the hair thingy she'd just bought would suit Alice's long, reddish-brown hair. "Hi, I thought you'd be up at Hartfell," she said.

"I will be – soon!" Alice held up her own bag. "Christmas pressies – almost finished!"

"Me too. I promised Jo I'd help clean tack this afternoon."

"But no rides today. I rang her. The ground's too icy."

Krista nodded. "I know."

"I offered to go up and do the tack too."

"Cool!" Krista grinned. "How are you getting up there? Do you want a lift?"

"That'd be great, thanks." Alice quickly phoned her mum to say she was driving up to the stables with Krista and her dad, then the two girls made their way through the crowds to the car park on the seafront.

"Hey, girls, hop in!" Krista's dad spotted them and opened his car door. "I take it you want me to run you straight up to the stables?"

"Please!" Alice sighed, settling happily back into her seat.

"Cool, Dad!" Krista looked ahead as the car crawled out into the traffic. Her Christmas shopping duty was done. Now she had the rest of the day ahead to enjoy the ponies at Hartfell!

"Though we have racing here today at Worcester, it has just been confirmed that there will be no meeting at York, and stewards are inspecting the course at Cheltenham." A commentator on TV explained how the freezing weather had affected the day's sport.

"It looks like ice and snow are pretty

widespread," Jo Weston remarked, walking into the tack room where Krista and Alice were busily polishing bits and stirrups to background noise from the telly. "At least we're not the only ones to suffer!"

Saturday was normally a busy time at Hartfell, when riders hacked out into the beautiful moorland countryside or down to Whitton Sands, or else took lessons from Jo in the arena. But today the frozen ground and icy surfaces had led to everything being cancelled.

"Yeah, and it means we can catch up here," Krista said. She stood back to admire the rows of shining metal. "I noticed Misty was missing a front shoe when I brushed her earlier. I added her to the list."

"Good. The blacksmith's due on Tuesday." Jo glanced up at the TV, perched on a wide shelf high on the wall. "Look at that chestnut mare!" she said with an admiring whistle.

Krista and Alice looked up at the screen.

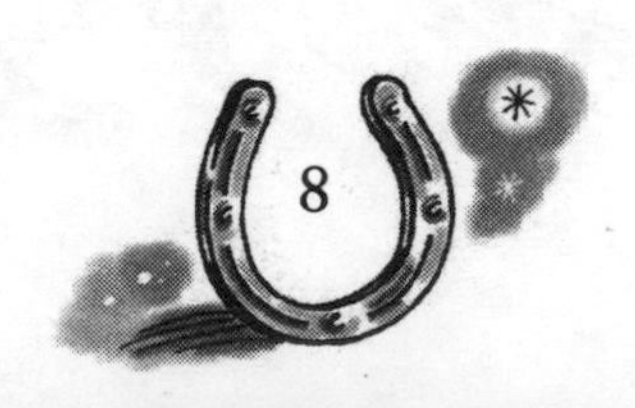

They were showing the runners on parade in the paddock before the next race. The chestnut which Jo had picked out was sleek and gleaming, groomed to perfection. And she stepped out on slender legs, prancing when her jockey mounted her then sidestepping impatiently towards the opening on to the racecourse.

"And this is the three to one favourite, Lady Madonna," the commentator said. "Trained by Martin Cornwell, ridden by Joe Miller."

"Gorgeous!" Alice sighed.

"And look at the grey!" Krista said. She'd spotted a runner called Night Watchman, also trained by Martin Cornwell, and picked him

as her own favourite because he looked like Apollo, Jo's own thoroughbred.

"I like the dark bay." Alice chose a horse called Don Juan, whose jockey wore a bright scarlet silk shirt and a black and white spotted hat.

For a few minutes Jo, Krista and Alice forgot the afternoon chores and watched the runners gather at the start. The ten horses bunched together, their jockeys holding them back until the starter gave them their orders, and then they were off, thundering down the track until they came to the first jump.

"Come on, Lady Madonna!" Jo called as her horse cleared the fence.

Krista saw Night Watchman fall a little

behind then catch up with the rest. Alice silently urged on Don Juan.

They sprinted on and jumped again, then again. Some slower horses began to trail behind. Don Juan took the lead after the sixth fence, with Lady Madonna second and Night Watchman back in fifth, still in with the leading bunch.

"My horse is going to win!" Alice cried, jumping up and down. "Come on, Don Juan!"

Krista's eyes were glued to the screen, her heart in her mouth at the idea that any one of the runners might fall at the next fence.

But all were clear and now there was only one fence to go. Don Juan was slowing down, Lady Madonna was overtaking him. The crowd roared her on.

Krista put her hand to her eyes and watched through the gaps in her fingers. Now she didn't care who won, as long as all the horses got back safely. Night Watchman flew over it and galloped for the finish line.

"And it's Lady Madonna, the favourite, winning by two lengths, with Don Juan in second place and Night Watchman coming in a very good third!" The commentator gave the results in a fast, high-pitched voice as the horses crossed the line. Sweat rose from them in white clouds. The winning

jockey, perched on his tiny saddle, leaned forward to pat his horse's neck.

"Phew!" Krista was glad the race was over. She loved the graceful racehorses, but hated to see them hit with whips and raced to their limits. "I'm off to make up the evening feeds," she told Jo. "Shall I give Misty and Drifter extra grass nuts?"

The stable owner nodded. "Alice, you can leave off here too and help me to bring the ponies in from the paddocks. It's going to be dark early tonight."

So the three of them left the tack room and braved the cold air, Krista heading for the feed bins, while Jo and Alice took head-collars out to the ponies. As she

scooped feed, Krista hummed happily.

Those thoroughbreds are brilliant athletes, she said to herself, *but they're nowhere near as cool as Misty and Drifter – or any of the ponies here at Hartfell, for that matter!*

She laughed at herself, hearing the ponies' hooves clip slowly across the yard. "OK, so I'm biased!" she said out loud.

Led by Alice, Misty came and poked her nose through the doorway of the feed room.

"She smells supper!" Alice laughed.

Krista left what she was doing and

went to stroke the strawberry roan pony's nose. "Are you hungry?" she murmured. "Do you want some yummy grass nuts?"

Misty blew warm air over Krista's hand. Then she turned her head to butt Alice's shoulder.

"Manners!" Alice warned, pushing her away then leading her on to her stable.

Krista went back to scooping. She breathed in the strong, sweet smell of the ponies' feed. *And those racehorses were definitely not in the same league as Shining Star!* she thought. For there was no horse or pony in the world to equal her magical pony, who lived far away in Galishe and was her very own secret friend.

Krista stopped, her feed scoop in midair,

eyes shining as she thought of the wonderful creature who arrived in this world in a cloud of silver light, his proud neck arched, his white mane flowing. Shining Star would call her to the magic spot on the cliff path overlooking Whitton Bay. He would appear in the sky and land at her side, folding his great wings, telling her that he needed her help. Krista would climb on to his back and they would fly to the rescue of ponies trapped by rising tides or children lost on the dark sands.

No, none of those horses on TV were anywhere near as cool as Shining Star! she thought with a smile, bending to pick up a bucket of grass nuts and carrying it out into the yard.

Chapter Two

Krista's boots crunched over the frosty grass. She walked quickly along the cliff path, planning to reach home well before dark.

Oops, I forgot my Christmas presents! she thought suddenly, about to turn on the narrow path and run back to the stables. *Oh no, I left them in Dad's car when he dropped Alice and me at Hartfell!* she recalled, marching on again. *Krista, you'd lose your head if it was loose!*

Laughing because she sounded like her teacher at school, she soon reached the tall rock to one side of the path which told her

that she'd arrived at Shining Star's magic spot, and though she'd been in a hurry, she stopped and took a good look around.

He won't come today, she thought, gazing up at the heavy grey sky. She hadn't had any sign that the magical pony needed her for a few weeks now, and she missed him. "I just stopped to say hello!" she murmured, studying the clouds, imagining for a moment that she saw a glimpse of silver and a break in the grey.

The wind was cold against her cheeks, and though every bit of her was wrapped up well, still her toes and fingers were freezing. Krista glanced over the sheer cliff towards the empty beach where white waves broke on the curving shore. Then she turned to stare up at

the moor, still hoping for a sprinkling of magic silver dust and a familiar voice calling her name.

No, there was nothing.

"Shining Star, hi, it's me – Krista!" she said, a tiny figure alone on the path.

Her voice was snatched from her lips and carried away by the wind. She waited, but there was no reply.

"Are you at home in Galishe?" she wondered out loud. "Are you resting with your brother, North Star, and your sister, Pale Moon?"

Krista stayed at the magic spot for as long as she dared, before the light faded and dusk fell. She walked round the tall rock, remembering the adventures she had had with Shining Star, running her gloved hand over the rough surface of the rock, gazing longingly at the sky. Krista alone held the secret of the magical ponies, and if anyone else saw them, they appeared as ordinary little moorland ponies with grey, shaggy coats and thick, tangled manes.

"Star, if you're too busy to come, I don't mind!" she whispered. "Just send me a message!"

She listened. Still there was nothing.

"Anything, just say my name to let me know you can hear me!"

There was no reply, only the wind whistling through the frozen bushes.

Krista tilted her head to one side. "OK, I give up," she said sadly, walking on to High Point Farm before darkness fell.

That evening Krista helped her mum decorate the Christmas tree. They brought down the box of lights and silver baubles from the loft and

carefully hung them on the spiky branches.

"I love this smell!" her mum sighed, breathing in the sharp scent of pine needles. "It reminds me of Christmases when I was a kid!"

Krista gazed into one of the silver balls,

seeing her own distorted reflection there. *This is when Christmas really starts,* she thought. But somehow this year she didn't have as much fun as usual decorating the tree, and as soon as it was finished, she yawned and said she would go to bed early.

"Huh?" her dad said, faking major shock.

"Did I hear that right?"

"I'm tired," Krista insisted.

"You get a good night's sleep," her mum said, giving her a hug.

"Early to bed!" Her dad shook his head in disbelief as Krista disappeared upstairs.

I wonder what's wrong with me, Krista thought as she lay in bed. It was gone midnight and her parents were in bed and sound asleep, but she'd lain awake for hours on end, staring out of the window at the dark, cloudy sky.

I don't feel ill. I'm not worried about anything. So what's going on?

She looked back over the last couple of days. The school term had ended on Friday

with a Christmas show. Krista had come home with a bag full of cards from friends which she'd arranged on the shelves and cupboards in her room. Then today she'd had a full morning of shopping followed by working with Alice and Jo at the stables. Perfect! So how come she couldn't get to sleep?

Her mind went back to the walk home from Hartfell – to the time when she'd stopped at the magic spot and thought of Shining Star.

That was it – the moment when her happy mood had changed. But why? Normally, thinking about her magical pony made Krista smile and feel excited, picturing him flying through the sky with his white wings spread wide, his mane flying back from his arched neck.

But not today. Today she'd been left with a frown, not a smile, and with a question that wouldn't go away. How come Star hadn't called her name and said hello when she'd asked him?

Lying in the darkness, Krista couldn't relax. *Just one word – my name or a greeting, just to say hi and Happy Christmas!*

And so the night passed and she was glad when morning came and she could throw herself into another day of working with the ponies at Hartfell.

Sunday saw more frost and ice. Once again Jo's lessons and rides were cancelled, and Krista worked indoors, getting the tack in good order.

Today, however, Alice didn't show up, and so it was just Jo and Krista.

"Are you looking forward to Christmas?" Jo asked, rubbing hard at a saddle to work saddle soap into the leather.

Krista stood nearby, reattaching reins to the polished metal bits. "Yep," she replied. "Mum and Dad have invited loads of people to our house on Boxing Day."

In the background, the TV was showing a football match.

"I know, I'm invited," Jo went on. "And on the day after Boxing Day I'm planning a big ride out to Arncliff Falls along bridleways and back lanes. It's open to anyone who wants to join in."

"Wow!" Krista liked the sound of this. "Can I help lead the ride?"

Jo nodded. "I'm counting on you being there."

On the TV, coverage of the football stopped for half-time and the link man read out some breaking news.

"We've just heard from our racing correspondent that two top horses have gone missing from Martin Cornwell's yard in

North Yorkshire. According to a local report, last year's Grand National winner, Lady Madonna and this year's Cheltenham Gold Cup winner, Night Watchman, were stolen overnight. Police are investigating and are asking people to come forward with any information that might help."

"Oh my!" Jo stopped what she was doing and shook her head. "Did you hear that, Krista?"

"Lady Madonna – she was the chestnut who came first in the race we watched yesterday!" Krista recalled the mare's beautiful gleaming coat and slender legs, and the way she'd run and jumped her heart out to win the race.

"My goodness, that horse must be worth millions of pounds!" Jo could hardly believe

what she'd just heard. As the TV commentator turned his attention back to football, she and Krista discussed the robbery. "And Night Watchman came third. He's one of the top steeplechasers around. Martin Cornwell has lost two of his best horses in one fell swoop!"

"But who would steal them?" Krista wondered. "It would need someone with a horse box. How can you sneak something as big as that into a stable yard?"

"I don't know. They didn't give many details. But the owners must be devastated, never mind the trainer."

"And why would the robbers want them?"

"For ransom money, I expect. This is like a kidnap, involving horses instead of people.

The kidnappers must think they can squeeze a lot of money out of the owners."

"Poor horses," Krista murmured. "I bet they were really spooked and scared!"

For a while they pictured the event, then Jo spoke up again. "Let's hope the police find them soon and get them safely back home."

Krista agreed. But the way Jo had spoken alarmed her. "You don't think the kidnappers will hurt the horses, do you?"

Jo shrugged and picked up her cloth, ready to begin work again. "I hope not, Krista," she said quietly. "But people who do this kind of thing can be pretty ruthless, believe me!"

Chapter Three

"Four days to go!" Krista's dad hummed a Christmas tune as he and Krista wrapped presents at the kitchen table.

This year Christmas Day fell on a Thursday, so Jo's big ride would take place on Saturday. As Krista folded and taped the wrapping paper, she thought of who she might ride.

Maybe Misty, she thought. *She'll have her new shoe by then. Or perhaps Drifter.* Drifter was a chestnut gelding who was a bit headstrong and needed a rider with a firm hand to keep him in check.

Running through the ponies at Jo's stable, Krista decided in the end that she didn't mind who she would ride. *They're all fun!* she told herself, putting the finishing touches to the wrapping.

"Did you read this?" Krista's mum popped her head around the door, holding up the evening paper. "About those two racehorses being kidnapped?"

Krista jumped up and took the paper from her. She read the headline – "DOUBLE WHAMMY! Two Top Horses Vanish from Training Yard."

"I saw it on the news," she muttered, carefully reading the front page report.

"Apparently it was cleverly done," Krista's

mum told her dad. "It seems that the theft took place somewhere en route from the racecourse to the stable yard. It was a two-hundred-mile journey and the driver of the horse box had to stop for fuel and so on. While he was away from his cab, the thieves opened up the back doors and switched horses!"

Krista read a section out loud. "Police suspect that Lady Madonna and Night Watchman were taken out of the horse box at the service station and replaced by two look-alikes –

a chestnut mare and a grey gelding. A spokesman from Westgate Manor Yard said that the operation had been carefully planned and the driver's suspicions were not aroused. He carried on with the journey and it was only when he arrived at the yard that anyone spotted the trick."

Krista's dad whistled through his teeth. "Those kidnappers had some nerve!"

"Anyway, I think it's awful." The more Krista learned about the kidnap, the worse it sounded. "I read in one of my horse books about this happening before to a horse called Shergar."

"Ah yes, Shergar," her mum said. "They never found that poor creature, did they?"

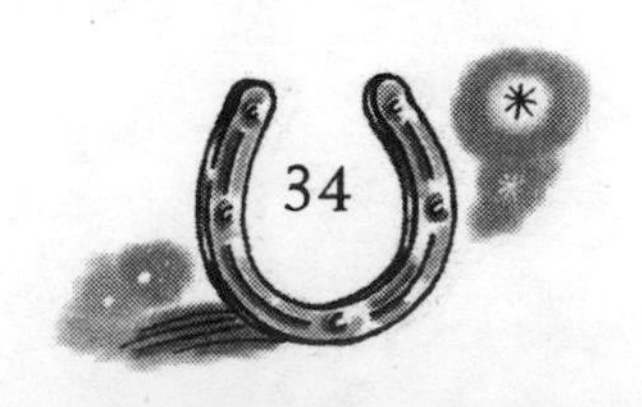

"Exactly!" Krista frowned. "The police looked for him all over Ireland, but they never solved the mystery."

"Yes, Shergar was a legend in his day," her dad said. "An absolutely brilliant horse, and worth a fortune. Ten million, I think they said, and that was more than twenty years ago."

"Like Lady Madonna and Night Watchman," Krista murmured, hoping with all her heart that this story would have a happier ending and that the two valuable horses would be found safe and well.

That night Krista had a dream. She'd fallen asleep easily, but had woken with a start, not once but twice, before her mum and dad had

come to bed and the house had fallen silent. Then Krista had slept again, but it had not been a peaceful sleep. Instead, she had a dream about the stable doors at Hartfell being left open and the ponies wandering out on to the frozen hillside. Then one about the two stolen racehorses speeding along a race track without riders, not stopping at the finish line but galloping through the crowd and out of sight.

Krista jerked half-awake, turned over on to her other side and slept again.

This time the dream lasted longer and was even more frightening. Shining Star appeared in the night sky, which had a strange orange glow, and beneath him the hillside was lit by

streetlamps. The magical pony circled, his silver glow pale against the weird orange light. Then Krista's dream jumped and the streetlights whirled and disappeared, replaced by darkness and the black shadows of tall trees, the sound of car engines roaring, hooves galloping and the wild neighing of horses.

There were two shapes galloping, plus a

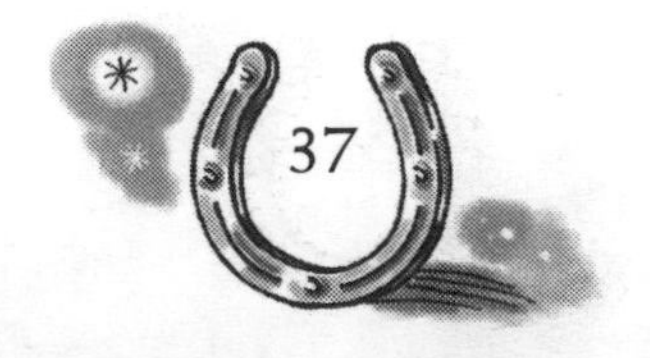

flash of silvery white. Ropes snaked through the air, horses crashed to the ground.

"We got them!" a triumphant voice cried.

Then there was total silence and darkness, and in the dream Krista herself tried to call for help, but no one heard, and there was Shining Star's muffled voice saying her name over and over – "Krista! Krista! Krista!"

She woke in terror and sat straight up in bed, her whole body shaking. Flinging back her duvet, she ran to the window and leaned out, searching the sky for her magical pony.

The sound of her footsteps must have woken her dad, because he soon came to her bedroom and found her standing at the window. "What happened?" he asked.

Krista turned to him with a look of terror. "I had a bad dream!"

"A nightmare," he soothed, taking her back to her warm bed. "Too much excitement during the day."

Still the horses' hooves drummed inside her head, and the sound of Shining Star's voice calling her name. She allowed herself to be tucked in. "Can I have a light on?" she pleaded in a small voice.

Her dad stroked her head and nodded. "It'll soon be morning," he promised. "Now do your best to settle down and rest."

Scared to go back to sleep, Krista waited until first light before she got up and dressed

in jeans and a thick jumper.

"Is that you, Krista?" her mum called from the bedroom next door. "Why are you up so early?"

"I just want to check on Spike!" Krista called back. Spike was her pet hedgehog, almost part of the family.

"Don't disturb him. Remember he's hibernating!"

"OK, I know." Spike had been the only excuse Krista could think of on the spur of the moment. "I want to check his nest-box."

"Put your jacket and boots on," her mum reminded her sleepily.

Downstairs, Krista wrapped herself up then stepped out into the yard. It was a clear

morning after days of unbroken cloud, and with the pale blue sky came a deep white frost covering the trees which lined the lane.

Instead of making for the front garden, where Spike's box nestled under a hawthorn hedge, Krista ran quietly into the lane and over the stile leading to the cliff path.

She headed straight for the magic spot and stood by the rock.

"Shining Star, it's me! I had a dream about you. A nightmare. Was it real?"

The wind whistled down the hill towards her, gusting past her and over the edge of the cliff towards the sea.

"Shining Star, can you hear me?"

Though she listened with all her might, Krista still heard nothing except the wind.

"The dream was about horses galloping through some dark trees. It didn't make sense, but you were in it and you were calling for me!"

More and more Krista was getting the feeling that something bad had happened to

Shining Star and that in some way it was linked with the two missing racehorses. She didn't know how exactly, and if she thought about it coolly it probably wouldn't sound sensible, but the nightmare had joined Star, Lady Madonna and Night Watchman together in her mind.

"Shining Star, are you OK?" she asked one last time.

And then, just as she was about to turn away and leave the magic spot, she did hear a voice – soft and low, reaching her between gusts of cold wind.

"Krista, I cannot come to the magic spot," Star's voice whispered. "I am kept in a prison without windows. The walls are thick."

"Oh, Shining Star, I knew something bad had happened!" Krista cried. She looked round helplessly, hoping against hope that he would appear.

"Listen! I am trapped with others and we need your help."

"What can I do?" she begged. The wind blew fiercely down the hillside, bringing storm clouds into the blue dawn sky. The first flakes of snow began to fall.

"You must be strong!" Shining Star warned. "And braver than you have ever been before."

"I will be!" Krista promised. Star's voice sounded fainter. The snow fell heavily.

"Come to me!" Shining Star said, his last words fading into the howling wind.

Chapter Four

Shining Star's words, "Come to me!" echoed inside Krista's head as she returned home.

How? she asked herself. *I don't have a clue where he is, and even if I did, how would I get there?*

The problem stayed with her as she had breakfast with her mum, after her dad had set off for work.

"Not hungry?" her mum asked, seeing Krista push away her dish of cereal.

She shook her head.

Her mum looked closely at her face and saw that she seemed pale and drawn.

"Not still bothered by that nightmare, are you?"

"No." Quickly Krista stood up and put on her jacket. "I told Jo I'd be at the stables by nine. I'd better get a move on."

"Are you sure you're OK?"

Krista stuck her feet into her boots. "I'm fine, Mum, honest!"

Unconvinced, Krista's mum stood at the kitchen door to watch her cross the yard. "Well, take care!"

Krista nodded and hurried on.

"Hey, Krista, what do you think about those racehorses being kidnapped?" The minute Krista arrived on the yard at Hartfell, Alice ran towards her, closely followed by Carrie Jordan.

The two girls had arrived early to help Jo muck out the stables.

Krista preferred not to discuss it, so she shrugged and walked on.

"Everyone's talking about it!" Carrie exclaimed. She was wearing a black baseball cap and a new, bright-pink jacket. "Early Christmas present," she explained, doing a twirl for the other two. "Do you like it?"

"Yeah, it's cool," Alice told her. "But, Krista, what about the kidnap?

Do you think the police will find the horses?"

Krista shrugged.

"It must be hard to hide two great big race-horses!" Carrie pointed out. "The police would have to be pretty stupid not to find them!"

"It depends." Krista didn't feel nearly so confident. "If the kidnappers are clever, they'll have planned it carefully and covered their tracks, like the thieves who took Shergar."

"Yeah, but neighbours would notice if there were two new horses around." Alice sided with Carrie. "They'd soon connect it with the kidnap 'cos it's in all the papers."

"Unless the kidnappers took them somewhere really far away and hid them out of sight." Krista had been thinking this

through during her walk to Hartfell. She'd remembered what Star had said about being held in a dark place. "Does anyone know if the kidnappers have asked for any money yet?"

"You mean a ransom demand?" Carrie was into the drama of the event, gasping as the three girls walked towards the tack room. "Oh wow, I wonder how much money they want!"

Inside, Jo was making a list of jobs for the day. She glanced up as the girls came in. "Hi, Krista, how are you doing?"

"Good, thanks." Krista spotted a newspaper on the table next to Jo's list. "Do you mind if I take a look at this?"

"Go ahead. If it's the missing racehorse story you're looking for, it's on page five."

Quickly turning the pages, Krista came to the one showing pictures of the famous steeplechasers under a headline which read, "Bookies Take Bets Against Finding Horse Superstars Alive!"

Krista's heart missed a beat. She read on. "Twenty-four hours after the dramatic seizure of two of racing's most successful steeple-chasers, police say there has still been no contact from the kidnappers and concerns are growing for the safety of Night Watchman and Lady Madonna.

"A police spokeswoman told our reporter that they had expected contact soon after the event and added, 'The more time that passes, the more reasons we have to be worried about

the welfare of these extremely valuable horses.'

"Their trainer, Martin Cornwell, told our reporter from his stable yard in North Yorkshire: 'The horses need to be returned as soon as possible. They are fed on a specialised diet and must be kept in conditions suitable for horses of this type,' he warned, adding, 'You can't just throw thoroughbred racehorses into any old stable with a pile of hay to keep them going.'"

You can't throw any horse into a stable without proper food and water! Krista thought. Her heart sank as she read the rest of the report, which gave more details of the theft from a service station on the M6, overlooking the Cumbrian Lakes. She read too that the police had

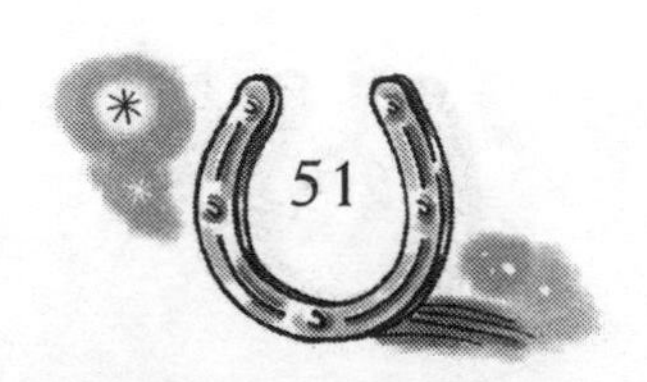

interviewed the driver of the horse box and released him without charge.

"So, what's happening?" Alice asked, as Krista folded the newspaper.

"Nothing. That's the problem." Krista wished the kidnappers would ask for money and get the whole thing over with.

"Well, there's no point standing around," Jo decided. "Carrie, can you take Comanche and Shandy out to the paddock? Alice, you take Drifter and Scottie. Krista, I'd like you to check Misty's feet – make sure the missing shoe hasn't made her lame."

Glad to be given a job and kept busy, Krista worked her way through the morning.

First she went to Misty's stable and picked

out her feet with a hoof pick. The grey pony stood patiently, lifting one foot at a time for Krista to inspect.

"Good girl!" Krista murmured, scraping carefully at the underside of each hoof. "You're so good. Yes, easy now!"

The pony's feet were sound, so Krista led her out to her paddock. Then she began to

muck out the empty stables, piling soiled straw into a barrow and wheeling it to an open trailer which would be driven out to one of the fields.

"Hot chocolate time!" Jo announced, appearing at the door of her house with a tray of steaming mugs.

Alice, Carrie and Krista drank eagerly.

"I just heard on the radio that the kidnappers have put in a ransom demand for two million!" Jo announced. "At least, that's what they're telling us."

"Two million!" Carrie echoed.

"Did they say anything else?" Krista wanted to know.

"No – no details. But things are moving."

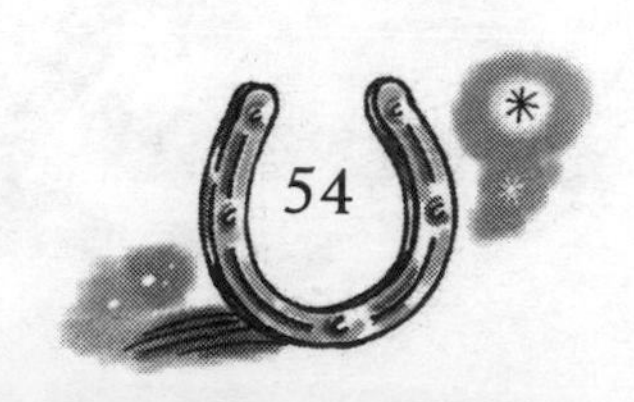

"Thank heavens," Alice said. "Who are the owners? Do you think they'll pay up?"

"They'd be mad not to," Jo replied. "Both Night Watchman and Lady Madonna are worth way more than that. Even if they never win another race, he'll go to stud and she'll become a brood mare. They'll earn their owners millions more in stud fees."

"But they'll have to hurry," Krista pointed out. "I reckon the trainer was right about having to look after them properly. And maybe these kidnappers don't know anything about horses. What if they're not giving them clean water to drink?"

"Trust you to worry about that," Carrie said. "I reckon they know what they're doing."

"Let's hope so," Jo said, taking her list of jobs out of her pocket and checking it. "That's it for the morning," she decided. "How about we all take the rest of the day off?"

It was midday as Krista made her way home along the cliff path. She was still feeling anxious about Shining Star, trailing the after-effects of her nightmare with her through the day. So when she came to the magic spot, she sighed and leaned back

against the tall rock, staring out to sea.

"I know, Star, I'm letting you down," she murmured sadly. "I can't think what to do next."

She longed for her magical pony to appear out of nowhere, for him to say that he and the kidnapped horses were safe and that he was flying home to Galishe to rest.

Krista recalled the words that Shining Star had spoken in her dream. "You must be strong, and braver than you have ever been before!" But she felt weak and helpless without him.

"What shall I do?" she asked, almost in despair. *Would her magical pony escape the danger he was in without her? Would she ever see him again?*

The day dragged on. Without chores at the stables, Krista's afternoon seemed endless.

"Cheer up, it's nearly Christmas!" her mum urged as she made pastry for mince pies. She asked Krista to spoon mincemeat into the small cases and to press the tops on each one. The mince pies went into a hot oven.

"It's not like you to be down in the dumps," her dad said after he got home from work that evening. He'd brought in a blast of cold air and a flurry of fresh snowflakes. "Unless one of the ponies at Hartfell is ill or something like that."

"Nothing's wrong," Krista insisted. She had promised her magical pony never to give away his secret – this was a problem she had to carry by herself.

"Star, come back and speak to me!" she

begged, opening her bedroom window when she went to bed that night. It was almost twenty-four hours since he'd appeared in her dream and her fears grew and grew. "It's never been like this before. Don't leave me to work it out by myself, please!"

The night sky was silent. A crescent moon shone down.

"What will Pale Moon and North Star say if you don't escape and go home to them?" Krista asked. "Think of them, Shining Star. Think of Galishe!"

Staring out of her window, Krista realised how anxious Star's sister and brother would be when he did not return. She thought of them standing in their peaceful home, surrounded

by silver-white light, wondering what had happened to their beloved brother.

Then Krista gasped. *North Star and Pale Moon – of course!*

Why hadn't she thought of it sooner? There were other magical ponies in Galishe besides her very own Shining Star. North Star, his older brother, strong and wise. Pale Moon, the younger sister, gentle and good. Surely one of those would come to help!

So Krista leaned eagerly out of the window, ignoring the cold winter air, concentrating on calling the magical ponies by name. "North Star, it's me, Krista. Your brother, Shining Star, is in trouble. He's been taken prisoner. Can you hear me?"

The moon shone pale gold, the stars twinkled over the snow-covered moor.

"Or Pale Moon, can *you* hear me? Your brother is trapped. I'm sure he was trying to stop a kidnap, but the thieves captured him too. Shining Star came to me in my dream!"

To Krista it seemed an endless wait without a reply. Finally she gave a heavy sigh and shook her head. No one was coming. Her idea had failed.

But then a small silver cloud drifted into sight. It floated across the moon, growing bigger. Krista held her breath. Was it just wishful thinking, or was the magical cloud really drawing nearer?

She watched and waited. The cloud glittered in the dark sky, growing brighter. Soon it hovered over the house, letting silver dust fall to the frozen ground until all that was left was the shape of a magnificent flying pony.

"Krista, I heard your call," North Star said in a deep, solemn voice. "Tell me, what is the matter? Where is my brother, Shining Star?"

"He's in danger!" Krista gasped out her reply. "North Star, we have to help him. I only hope we're in time!"

Chapter Five

Krista stood at her bedroom window, half-afraid.

North Star seemed more serious than Shining Star, and more stern. There was a proud look in his eye. Yet he had the same glittering appearance as her magical pony. His white coat sparkled and shimmered with a soft silver light.

"Describe the danger my brother is in," he said, hovering close to the silent house.

"I don't know exactly." Krista began shyly. "But I think he's trapped – held prisoner with

two other horses. At least that's how it seemed in my dream."

North Star tilted his head to one side. "Tell me more."

Surrounded by the magical pony's silver mist, Krista felt herself relax. "Star spoke to me but he didn't appear. Lots of things were happening – horses galloping, a man shouting, and Star's voice telling me he was trapped in a place without windows."

North Star listened carefully. "Did he tell you where he was?"

Krista shook her head. "No, his voice faded away and I woke up. I'm sorry – it's not much to go on."

"Who are the other horses in your dream?"

North Star asked. He sounded calm and alert to everything that Krista told him.

"Lady Madonna and Night Watchman. They're racehorses." Eagerly, Krista told North Star all she knew about the kidnap.

North Star listened then glanced around, looking for a spot to land. "Will you come with me to the place where the horses were stolen?" he asked.

"You mean, fly with you?" She looked down at her pyjamas. "Can I get dressed first?"

North Star nodded. "I will wait for you in the field below the house. There is no time to lose. Hurry."

Taking a deep breath, Krista rushed to put on her jeans and sweatshirt. Then she picked

up her boots and jacket and crept downstairs, past the living room where the TV played loudly. She tiptoed into the kitchen, pausing to put on her boots. Then she opened the door and dashed outside.

Only then did she dare to breathe again, slipping round the side of the house and into the garden where she saw a soft silver glow in the field below. She soon came to North Star. "It's a long journey," she warned. "The place where the kidnap happened is hundreds of miles away."

North Star nodded and bade her come closer. "I see lakes and mountains covered in mist," he murmured. "I see a long,

wide road with many cars."

"That's it – a motorway!" Always amazed by the magical ponies' gift of seeing things that were invisible to normal sight, Krista grew braver. "Shall I climb on your back now?" she asked.

"Wait." North Star spread his white wings then nodded. He raised his head and looked far into the distance.

So Krista climbed astride his broad back and took hold of his silky mane. She felt North Star beat his wings, slowly at first as they rose from the ground, then faster, to take them high above the field and flying over the moor towards Whitton Bay.

Once more Krista held her breath. The

wind rushed against her face, the moon and stars shone over her head as she and North Star flew over the sea, faster and faster, until the waves seemed to whirl up over their heads and the stars glittered beneath their feet, so that everything in the world changed places and they sped through a tunnel of glittering darkness into a silvery blue light.

Krista and North Star emerged in broad daylight beside a vast, half-frozen lake that stretched to rugged mountains in the far distance.

"Where are we?" Krista asked. They soared over the water towards the mountains.

"We are close to the road which carries cars

past the mountains in a never-ending chain," North Star explained. "We have travelled through time into tomorrow so that our search does not take place in the dark."

"Wow!" In spite of her fears for Shining Star, Krista couldn't help feeling a shiver of pure excitement. "Look at the frozen surface! Half the lake is covered in ice!"

"And the mountains are capped with snow." North Star took her closer to the peaks, which sparkled pure white. The surface of the snow was untouched, drifting into hollows and softening the sharp outline of the rocks.

"Cool!" Krista gasped, crouching low to shelter from the worst of the biting wind.

She grasped North Star's mane with both hands, feeling the magic of each moment as he turned and swooped back towards the lake.

"Now we must find the road," North Star said, rising high into the air again and clearing another range of snowy hills.

Below Krista saw another, smaller lake, and beyond that, hills rolling as far as the eye could see. "In my dream there was an orange glow coming from a town in the distance."

"There!" North Star tilted his wings and flew in the direction of a cluster of stone houses set against a hillside.

"Yes, this must be it." Krista saw that it was the only town nearby. "And look – there's

the motorway running alongside."

North Star slowed down as they reached the town. He flew low over the slate roofs and narrow streets and at last hovered over the broad lanes of traffic whizzing below.

"They go so fast!" Krista breathed. The bird's eye view of the cars scared her. Windscreens glinted in the sun. Red, silver, blue and black shapes hurtled on.

"How could thieves steal horses here?" North Star asked. Puzzled, he looked up and down the motorway at the endless stream of traffic.

"They did it at a service station – a place where you stop for petrol. Look, over there, where the cars are in that big car park!"

Once the magical pony understood, he beat his wings again and flew towards the services, steering clear of the parked cars and landing on open moorland beyond the café area. "Good!" he said, pricking his ears to all the sounds. "Now, Krista, it is time for you to find out more."

"OK, what do you want me to do?" Slipping from his back, she turned to face the service station. Her legs felt shaky after the amazing journey, but her head was clear.

"Do what I cannot do," North Star explained. "Go and ask questions. Find out as much as you can."

"And you'll wait here?" she checked. She noticed something about their surroundings

that puzzled her. "You know there are no trees around," she said, pointing out the bleak, open hillsides stretching in all directions. "There were tall, dark trees in my dream, and the horses were galloping through them."

North Star nodded but said nothing.

"Will you look for tracks while I'm at the service station?"

He nodded again. "The ground is frozen, so clues will be hard to find. Still, I will search."

So Krista left North Star and set off through the frozen heather. Hoping not to be seen,

she climbed a fence at the back of the huge car park and walked quickly past petrol pumps towards the low building beyond.

She went straight in to the busy café area, past signs for toilets, past noisy games machines, towards a shop selling newspapers and sandwiches, where she stopped and looked around.

How do I do this? she wondered, standing close to the newspaper stand. *Who do I ask? Who'll want to talk to me? I'm only a kid!*

She stood uncertainly for a while, watching people pick up newspapers and take them to the till.

This is Tuesday, she thought, remembering that North Star had flown through time.

Then she glanced at a newspaper to see if there was more news about the horses. Sure enough, Lady Madonna and Night Watchman had hit the headlines again.

"£2 Million Gamble Fails!"

Krista grabbed a paper and read the report. "Owners Pay Ransom but Racehorses Are Not Returned!" She sighed and shook her head.

"Can you believe this?" A customer spoke to the woman at the till. He stabbed at the headline with his forefinger. "The kidnappers grabbed the money and ran!"

The woman nodded. "I know. It happened here last night. I wasn't on duty, but I heard the police made a mess of the handover of the cash. It doesn't look good for those poor horses."

"Were you here on Saturday, when it all kicked off?" The nosey customer did Krista's job for her. Krista stood close by and took in every detail.

"Yes, I actually sold a newspaper and a can of Coke to Bill Greenaway, the driver of the horse box. I recognised his picture in the paper next day." The chatty woman was obviously eager to talk about her involvement in the big story. "He's a little chap – an ex-jockey himself. But there's a funny thing about all this ..."

"What?" Krista couldn't help herself – she jumped right into the middle of the conversation.

The woman behind the till raised her

eyebrows then laughed. She went back to gossiping with the customer. "It's true, Bill Greenaway did nip in to buy stuff. But he was only here a couple of minutes, then he went straight back out and set off on the road again. I watched him go."

"So what?" the customer asked.

Krista was way ahead of the man. "So there was no time to open up the horse box and switch horses!" she cried. "It means someone's been lying all along!"

Chapter Six

Out on the exposed moor, Krista and North Star talked it through. "A lot of things are not right around here," Krista insisted. "Don't you feel that too?" There were no trees and no tracks, plus there was no time to have done the kidnap.

The magical pony agreed. "I don't believe my brother came here. I cannot sense his presence."

Krista frowned. "So maybe I was wrong all along – Shining Star didn't try to rescue Lady Madonna and Night Watchman after all!"

"Perhaps," North Star murmured thoughtfully. "But I would like to visit their stable yard in any case."

Krista climbed on to North Star's back and told him the name of the stable yard. "It's in North Yorkshire. I think there are loads of racing yards around there, so we'll have to find the right one."

North Star listened then beat his wings. They rose quickly above the service station and the motorway which had given them so few clues.

"Are we going to land in daylight?" Krista asked, crouching down low and holding tight. She felt the magical pony soar high into the sky, then took one last look at the wonderful frozen lakes below.

"No. We will seek the cover of darkness," North Star replied.

So Krista made herself ready for the journey back. She felt the land beneath her tilt as North Star gathered speed. They were surrounded by glittering dust, tilting further until the world began to whirl and they entered a shining tunnel of light.

"Wow, cool!" Every time Krista flew with the magical ponies, she was thrilled. It was like the best theme park ride in the world. No, it was so wonderful it was like nothing else on earth!

Soon, the silvery tunnel opened out into darkness. The world stopped spinning and North Star hovered over a dark hillside.

Krista studied the new scene. In the pale moonlight she could make out soft, rolling hills broken by small patches of woodland and dotted with lights from scattered farms. "Is this it?" she murmured, still dazed by the magic flight.

"A town lies beyond that high hill," North Star replied. "The stable we seek is nearby."

"And you think that Shining Star has been here?" Already Krista had picked up a new, strained tone in North Star's voice. His ears flicked this way and that, he breathed deep and flared his nostrils.

"Perhaps," he said warily. "Let us go and find out."

So they circled the hills, dipping low to

discover the yards belonging to the racehorse trainers, spotting two or three houses surrounded by stable blocks and large paddocks before North Star finally stopped above a grand manor house backing on to a big yard lined with rows of stables. Beyond the stables was a large covered arena, and beside that was a round pool whose water glittered in the moonlight.

"Maybe ..." North Star said, still cautious.

"Fly to the entrance," Krista suggested. She felt sure there would be a notice by the gate giving the owner's name.

Sure enough, when North Star flew low enough for her to see, she read out the words they were hoping for. "'Westgate Manor

Stables. Proprietor: M. Cornwell.' Yes, this is it!"

Relieved, North Star landed inside the main gates. Within the large grounds, all was quiet. There were no lights on in the house, and the stable block was lit only by dim safety lamps.

Krista took the lead as she and North Star trod quietly across the front lawns, through a brick arch into the yard. "What wonderful stables!" she whispered, taking in the neat, stone-flagged yard and the shiny black stable doors. She peered into the one nearest to the entrance, making out a large bay thoroughbred in an immaculate purple and green rug. The horse raised its head and came to greet her by poking its head over the door.

"Hush!" North Star warned. He led the way

around the side of the stable block and stood by the round pool.

"Look, it's a swimming pool for horses!" Krista exclaimed. She ran on to the ramp which stretched over the water and which would lower the horse into the pool. "Wow – I mean, what cool exercise!"

But North Star was hardly listening to her. "Something is wrong," he warned. "Listen,

Krista, I want you to run back into the yard and read the names of the horses on the stable doors. When you come to the stables of the missing horses, take a good look inside."

Krista nodded and quickly retraced her steps. She stopped at the corner of the yard to listen out, heard nothing and ran on from one stable to the next.

At each door she read the label and peered inside. True Love was a tall, black gelding with a long, sleek neck and a white star on his forehead. Autumn Gold was a chestnut. The label on her door said that she was a five-year-old. And so on, around the yard.

Krista was bewitched by the horses' beauty. "You're gorgeous!" she whispered

again and again, tearing herself away. "You're so pretty! I love your face – it's beautiful!"

The horses stared back at her, wondering why this stranger was here at their stable door in the middle of the night.

But where was Lady Madonna's stable? And where had Night Watchman lived before he had been kidnapped? Krista had almost come to the end of the last row.

Across the yard, one of the racehorses – Autumn Gold – came to her door and neighed loudly. Krista turned with a start. "It's OK, it's only me!" she whispered, creeping on regardless. She came at last to an empty stable without a label on the door. She looked inside at a bed of clean wood shavings, then

went on and peered over the next door. This was the same as the one before – empty, but with a clean bed as if ready for a new arrival.

Two empty stables. Two missing horses. OK, that made sense. But why had they taken away the name plates so soon? Had Martin Cornwell already accepted that

Night Watchman and Lady Madonna wouldn't return?

Krista's thoughts were broken by a second horse neighing from his doorway and a light going on in a small room tucked away in one corner of the yard. She froze where she was, beside the empty stable.

A door opened and a figure appeared. "Hey, Autumn, what's up?" a girl's voice said.

Krista pressed herself back against the wall, watching as the tall, fair-haired girl, dressed in tracksuit bottoms and a T-shirt, walked towards the chestnut mare.

The girl checked Autumn Gold's stable then stroked her neck. "What spooked you? Was it a fox?"

Krista bit her lip. She began to sidle towards the end of the row, praying that she could reach it before the stable girl turned and saw her.

"It's not like you, Autumn!" the girl went on. "You go back inside and get some sleep, you hear!"

Krista made it to the corner and slid into the darkness round the side of the building. She could hear the girl's footsteps returning down the row of stables at the far side, then the click of a door.

Wait five minutes for it to be safe! Krista told herself. She stayed where she was until the yard fell quiet. *OK, now there must be a back way!*

Staying clear of the yard, Krista made her

way in the darkness around the back of the stable buildings and the big covered arena, treading over grass and rocks until she came to the exercise pool where North Star waited.

"Well?" he asked, breathing a silvery cloud into the cold air. "I heard a voice. What happened?"

"A stable girl came out and almost caught me," Krista admitted. "But I did get chance to look into two empty stables where the kidnapped horses must have lived. It was weird – they've taken their names off the doors already."

"But now it's too dangerous to go back and take another look," North Star decided. "Besides, the sky is growing light in the east.

Before long, the people of the house will be awake."

"And my mum and dad will be getting up and calling me for breakfast," Krista remembered.

"It is time to go," North Star said. "We have learned enough."

"What have we learned?" she asked, climbing on to his back. It was true, the sun was rising, casting long shadows over the hillside.

"That people are lying," the magical pony replied as he spread his wings and flew Krista back home. "That there is danger in the air, and all is not as it seems!"

Chapter Seven

OK, we're stuck! Krista went over the events of last night time and time again, ignoring her mum, who was ironing a shirt for her dad. *North Star and I have followed up all the clues we had – at the motorway services and at Westgate Manor – and we came up against a dead end!*

"Krista?" her mum interrupted. "Did you hear what I said?"

Krista waited for her toast to pop up out of the toaster. "No, sorry. What?"

"I said, there's bad news about those two racehorses. The owners paid the ransom but

the kidnappers didn't hand them over."

"I know!" Krista sighed, caught unawares.

Her mum gave her a funny look. "How come?"

"Hmm?"

"How come you already knew about the ransom? You've only just crawled out of bed."

"Oh. No, I didn't mean, I knew. I didn't know. I mean, that's awful news!" Krista went red and rushed out of the room.

"What's Krista on about now?" her dad asked her mum, catching the jumbled, mumbled words as he came into the kitchen for his shirt.

Her mum shook her head and unplugged the iron. "Search me. We were talking about those racehorses and she kind of lost the plot!"

"I sometimes wonder about our daughter!" Krista's dad shook his head, taking the shirt and putting it on. "I'm sure she wouldn't be so upset if it had been mere humans who'd been kidnapped!"

"Don't make fun." Krista's mum followed him to the foot of the stairs. "It said on the news that the handover of the ransom took place at midnight at the service station, but apparently the police moved in too soon, before the horses could be handed over. The kidnappers suspected a trap, grabbed the money and drove off."

Upstairs in her room, Krista heard the details and her heart sank.

"So what will they do with the horses now?"

her dad wondered. "I don't suppose they'll just let them go."

"No way," her mum agreed. "My guess is the kidnappers will want to get rid of the evidence as soon as possible."

Krista's stomach somersaulted and her legs went shaky. *Get rid of the evidence! Oh no!*

"Hush!" her dad warned, noticing that Krista's door was open.

Get rid of the evidence! That suggested only one thing. Krista sat down heavily on her bed. *The kidnappers are going to kill Lady Madonna and Night Watchman. And, without me, Shining Star won't be able to stop them!*

*

As soon as she could, Krista left the house and made her way to the magic spot.

"Don't be late back from the stables!" her mum had called as she dashed out of the door. "Remember we're going to the Christmas concert in town tonight!"

Krista ran on. The last words that North Star had said to her when they parted in the dawn light were, "Return to the magic spot as soon as you are able. I will be waiting."

Please be there! Krista thought as she climbed the stile and ran on along the cliff path. Now that she knew the horses were likely to be killed, her heart raced and her mind whirled with a hundred scary thoughts.

Her feet crunched over the frosty ground.

But there was no North Star waiting by the tall rock, and though the sky was filled with heavy clouds, there was no silver light or any sign of the magical pony.

Lost in troubling thoughts, Krista crouched beside the rock, hugging her knees to her chest, so that she didn't see the silver mist surround her and fall softly on her dark head.

"Krista!" Shining Star's voice was weak, his light dim.

She looked up and gasped, hardly recognising what she saw. Star had appeared like a shimmering ghost, his shape wavering above her head, fading, growing brighter then fading again.

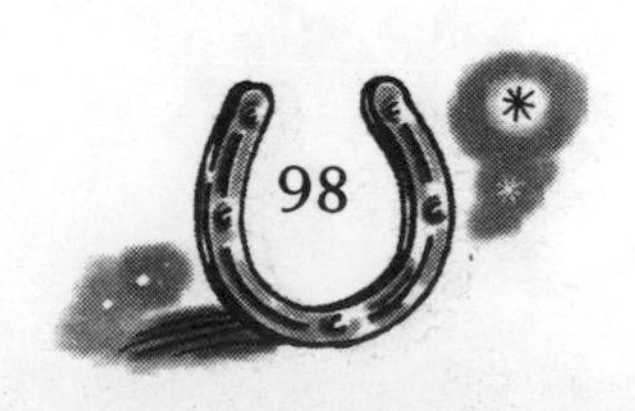

"The danger is great," he warned. "It is closing in on us, hour by hour."

"Oh!" Krista sprang to her feet. "North Star came to help. We searched for you yesterday, but we couldn't find you. We don't even know where you are!"

"Keep searching," Star implored, his light growing dimmer and his image fading into the grey sky until only his face remained. "Lady Madonna is weak. Night Watchman has been beaten ..."

Krista put her hands to her mouth. "Tell me where you are!" she begged.

But Shining Star had used all his strength.

He faded from view. "Be brave!" his voice told her. "Come before it is too late!"

After Shining Star had gone, Krista waited for what seemed like an age. She paced helplessly along the frozen path. With every step she grew more desperate, wondering what had happened to North Star, until finally she looked up to see a bright silver cloud break through the mass of grey and float towards her. *At last!*

She ran to the spot, looking up as a sprinkling of silvery dust showered the ground. "North Star, where have you been?" she demanded, even before the magical pony appeared.

"I flew to Galishe to give them news," he explained. "My father and sister grow afraid for Shining Star. I told them we would find him and I would bring him home."

By now Krista could make out the full shape of the winged pony, who had flown back to her through the heavens faster than the speed of light. His silver glow was strong, and he held his head high. "Shining Star tried to reach me, but he was too weak," she told North Star. "He told me it was almost too late!"

"Then we must hurry," North Star said, hardly waiting for Krista to climb on his back before he spread his wings and took off again.

"Now we know for sure that Shining Star is trapped with Lady Madonna and Night

Watchman," Krista said as they flew high above Whitton Bay. "Star told me so himself."

"I had no doubt," North Star replied, gaining speed and entering the whirling tunnel of silvery light that would take them back to Westgate Manor. "I did not feel my brother's presence by the wide road by the lake, but I felt it in the hills close to the trainer's yard. That is why we return there to search again."

Krista sat quietly, trusting North Star to take them quickly to Martin Cornwell's yard, glad when she could look down through grey clouds at the grand house and stable yard. "Yes, this is the right place," she said, noticing the covered arena and round pool. She saw too that cars had parked outside the main gates and

a small knot of people had gathered.

"Quickly then!" North Star chose a place to land, out of sight of the yard. "Go and find out all you can."

Krista nodded. She did not stop to think or grow scared as she ran towards the gates. "What's happening?" she asked the first person she came to – a man in a black leather jacket, with a camera slung around his neck.

The photographer shrugged. "Nothing yet. We're waiting for a statement from Cornwell."

"Are you all journalists?" Krista asked, noticing more cameras.

The man nodded. "This is a big story. Front page news. We want to know what went wrong with the handover of the loot."

"Any news of the horses?" Krista asked, trying to sound like some kid who was just passing by.

"Not yet."

Krista shuddered and slipped away, past the gates and round the outside of the garden wall. With a bit of luck, they were all so busy concentrating on the front drive that no one would see her.

So far so good – she'd reached a small wood that ran up the hill from the back of the

covered arena and she decided to use the trees to hide behind. She hadn't paid them much attention in the darkness of her first visit, but now she found it easy to slip quietly through the shadows until she came to the corner of the arena and spotted a narrow gap between it and the pool. She ventured down the gap on to the edge of the yard.

Now what? Krista could see the stables with the horses peering over the doors. She heard footsteps and voices, saw a stable lad carrying buckets of feed. There were giant bales of hay stacked in one corner of the yard, and Krista chose this as a place to hide. She waited until the yard was empty, then dashed across and squatted behind the bales, her heart thumping.

She'd made it into the heart of Martin Cornwell's training yard!

"Georgie, can I have a word?" A man's voice shouted from the doorway of what could be a tack room.

From her hiding place, Krista saw the tall, blonde girl from the night before appear from one of the empty stables. In the daylight she looked pale and sad.

"No point moping about in there," the man said harshly. He was small, with wiry red hair, and stepped out to meet Georgie with an unpleasant scowl. "You've got work to do!"

"I'm upset, Bill," Georgie told him. "I can't believe Lady Madonna might never come back!"

"Yeah well, get over it."

The stable girl hung her head. "It's not that easy. I've looked after Madonna ever since she arrived. I know every little thing about her."

"Well, it doesn't pay to get too attached in this job," the man reminded her. "We're looking after expensive horseflesh, that's all!"

Ouch! From behind the bales Krista winced, wondering if this was Bill Greenaway, who'd been driving the horse box when the horses had been kidnapped.

His cruel words made Georgie break down in tears.

"Oh for goodness' sake!" he muttered, striding back towards the tack room. "Pull yourself together and clear the rest of the stuff out of Lady Madonna's stable."

As he walked back and left Georgie crying, Krista saw another man come on to the yard.

She knew at a glance that this must be Martin Cornwell himself from the way he dressed and acted, strutting out of his office in a crisp pale blue shirt and dark trousers, looking as if he was about to give orders to anyone who crossed his path. He quickly spotted Bill Greenaway. "Bill, I need you to come into town with me. The police want to take our statements!" he yelled.

"I'll be right there, Mr Cornwell!"

Greenaway called, giving Georgie a final warning. "Shut it! No one wants to see you moping around the place! And don't speak to the journalists – not a word, OK!" Then he hurried across to join his boss.

Krista held her breath, waiting for the men to get into a car and leave the yard before she dared to peer out from behind the bales.

Then she took a big decision. After all, what could she lose? She stood up and walked out from her hiding place.

"Hey, where did you spring from?" Georgie asked, wiping her wet cheeks when she saw Krista. "Kids aren't supposed to come in here."

"I know. I'm sorry you're sad," Krista said quietly. "It must be awful to lose Lady Madonna."

Georgie nodded and broke down again. "Honestly, I can't believe it. Madonna is like my baby. She's beautiful. I just want her back!"

"I saw her race on Saturday. She's gorgeous," Krista agreed. "And Night Watchman."

"Him too. But I didn't look after him. That was Bill's job. Night Watchman's gone, Bill just seems to brush it to one side. I don't know how he does that!"

"I know how you must feel," Krista said, letting the stable girl cry all she wanted. She'd obviously bottled things up and now it was all spilling out.

"And he didn't even show any emotion on the day it happened. He unloaded the horse box late on Saturday, and it was me who

spotted that the horses had been switched. Bill didn't even seem to care!"

"Didn't you travel down to the racecourse with them?" Krista asked.

Georgie shook her head. "No, I stayed here. Mr Cornwell drove down with Bill that day, but he didn't come back with him. I guess he stayed down to celebrate the win."

"And they were definitely different horses?" Krista checked. She knew that soon Georgie would pull herself together, as Greenaway had ordered, and she would realise that she shouldn't be discussing this with a stranger.

"Yeah, totally different," Georgie sniffed. "They were cross-breeds – OK, a chestnut

and a grey, but nothing like our two thoroughbreds."

"But Bill didn't seem to mind? What about Mr Cornwell?"

"He was pretty calm about it too," Georgie recalled. "He arrived early Sunday morning, when the police were already here, and I expected major fireworks from him. He can

explode big-time when he wants to."

Krista nodded. "Weird," she muttered. "But maybe he kept calm because he wanted to help the police."

Georgie shook her head. "No," she said. "He didn't get angry, he didn't even look surprised. I didn't understand it at the time."

"And do you now?" Krista saw the other stable worker come on to the yard and knew that her time with Georgie was definitely up.

"Yeah, I get it," the girl said bitterly. "I know now that Martin Cornwell doesn't care about the horses here. And I'll tell you something else – as soon as he gets back from town, I'm going to go into his office and quit!"

Chapter Eight

Krista left the stable yard before Georgie and the stable lad could begin asking her awkward questions. She found North Star where she had left him, in a field beside the small wood.

"This is the weirdest thing!" she cried. "I've managed to talk to Lady Madonna's groom and she's really upset, like you'd expect. But Martin Cornwell, who should really, *really* care about what's happened, isn't the least bit bothered. I caught a glimpse of him, and honestly, he didn't seem like a very nice man!"

North Star listened and nodded. His own

earlier suspicions were confirmed. "Nothing is as it should be," he said quietly.

Krista stopped to take a deep breath. "This is going to sound stupid," she warned, glancing at the dark shadows in the wood and then up the long, open hillside beyond. Stone walls made a kind of frosty green patchwork, broken by scattered hawthorn trees and stone barn buildings. "But I'm thinking maybe Lady Madonna and Night Watchman weren't actually kidnapped at all!"

The magical pony nodded, letting his long, silky mane fall over his serious face. "Say more," he prompted.

"Well, say, for instance, somebody wanted to make it look like a kidnap, as if some

thieves who didn't really exist had suddenly come and stolen the horses from the service station, but really it was an inside job ..."

"... Meaning?"

"Meaning, it was planned by Martin Cornwell himself, and he used Bill Greenaway as his accomplice. Between them they invented the story about the kidnap!"

"But why would he do that?"

"To get the ransom. The owners handed over two million pounds, remember!"

Once more North Star nodded. "It would explain why we picked up no clues on the road by the lake," he agreed. "And why I feel that nothing seems right here at Westgate Manor."

"And look, those could be the trees I saw in my dream!" Krista pointed urgently to the nearby wood. "I'm certain Martin Cornwell and Bill Greenaway transferred the horses to another horse box themselves, not at the motorway services, but somewhere close to here. Night Watchman and Lady Madonna tried to escape when Cornwell was about to hide them. That's

when Shining Star arrived to help."

"But all three were captured." North Star gazed gravely up the hillside. "If this is true, Cornwell is a greedy deceiver," he muttered.

"What shall we do?" Krista knew that time was running out. When she'd talked to Shining Star that morning, his strength was almost spent.

"Perhaps Cornwell still intends to free the horses." North Star was lost in his own thoughts.

"I don't think so. Maybe he never had any intention of letting them go. Shining Star told me that Night Watchman had been beaten and Lady Madonna was weak."

"Then he is more ruthless than I had

believed possible." North Star shook his head. "Where is this man now, Krista?"

"He drove into town with Bill Greenaway."

"We will follow them," North Star decided.

Krista climbed on his back, her nerves too strung out to notice the ground slip away as the magical pony spread his wings and rose into the air. "We have to hurry!" she whispered, feeling the cold air rush by, hardly seeing the fields to either side as North Star flew swiftly and followed the road into town.

When they reached the houses gathered around an old, cobbled market square, the magical pony slowed and hovered over the gleaming cars parked below. "Which one belongs to Cornwell?" he asked.

Krista looked hard and at last spotted the silver Range Rover which she'd seen in the yard at Westgate Manor. "There!" she murmured, looking round the square at an old-fashioned pub, a church and a row of shops beside a small police station with police cars parked outside.

People came and went, in and out of the shops, standing in the square to talk and pass the time of day.

"So the men are still here," North Star concluded. "Krista, you must dismount and wait here until they return to their car."

"Where will you be?" she asked, holding her breath as he flew to the churchyard and dipped low for her to drop to the ground.

"I will wait here," he promised.

So Krista nodded and ran back, between the old, moss-covered gravestones, through the iron gates on to the square. She was just in time to see Cornwell and Greenaway emerge from the police station.

The two men walked to their car then stood, deep in conversation. Krista crept nearer, hanging about beside first this car then that, managing at last to come within earshot.

"You did a good job, Bill," Cornwell was saying. "You remembered our story word for word."

Greenaway grinned.

"I'd rehearsed it a few times before I made the statement, Mr Cornwell!"

The trainer smirked. "These dumb country cops are never going to be clever enough to pick holes in our alibis. Besides, I think they know they shouldn't have stepped in so fast when the money was changing hands last night. The horse owners are going to come down on them hard for that!"

"But it worked out well for us," Greenaway said. "It was no problem for me to snatch the bags of cash from the fuel area and make a quick getaway while everyone panicked and made a mess of things."

Krista crouched behind a car, listening to every word. *I was right!* she thought. *There was*

no kidnap. These two did it themselves. And they think they've got away with it!

"Like I said, good job!" Taking his car keys from his jacket pocket, Cornwell unlocked the car. "Now there's only one little thing left to take care of."

Greenaway nodded.

"It'll take two of us." The trainer sounded casual, as if he was talking about changing a light bulb. "One to hold the horse, one to give the injection."

"You can count on me," Greenaway assured his boss.

Cornwell nodded and got in the car. "Then let's get on with it," he said, slamming the door.

They're going to kill the horses! Krista realised.

Unless we can stop them, they're going to do it now, right this minute!

North Star flew low, keeping pace with the silver Range Rover.

They followed them for a mile or two up a country lane, heading back towards Westgate Manor. But when Cornwell came to the turn-off to his house, he ignored it. Instead, he drove straight on until he came to a narrow back lane, no more than a rough track, which led behind the wood overlooking the stable yard then wound on up the hill towards the rolling horizon.

Her heart thumping, her hands grasping North Star's mane, Krista remembered her

magical pony's words. *You must be strong. You must be braver than you have ever been before!* This was life and death – they had to save two beautiful horses and her own Shining Star!

Cornwell drove on, leaving the wood behind, following a grass track up the hill, passing bare hawthorns bent by the constant winds, driving straight past the first stone barn they reached.

"Where is he going?" Krista muttered.

Ahead was more open country. She stared at an isolated barn standing on the top of the hill. "Unless … That's it!" she decided, urging North Star on ahead of the Range Rover.

The magical pony beat his wings faster and flew ahead, dropping quickly to the ground at the far side of the barn. Krista dismounted, stumbling in her haste to beat Cornwell and Greenaway and find the horses.

"My brother, we are here!" North Star called, his sixth sense telling him that they had found the place where Shining Star was being held prisoner.

The door to the barn faced away from the wind, overlooking the valley where Westgate Manor stood. There were no windows, no

daylight penetrating the thick stone walls.

Krista tried the door. "It's locked!" she cried, tugging at the big padlock. She ran to the corner of the barn and glanced down the track to see Cornwell's Range Rover approaching fast. "We'll have to hide and let them unlock it!"

"Then we will take them by surprise," North Star promised, preparing to step out from behind the barn.

So they kept out of sight until the car arrived. They heard the slam of two car doors and footsteps crunch over the frozen ground. Fear choked Krista as she listened to the turn of a key in the padlock.

"Now!" North Star said.

They stepped out just as Cornwell opened the door wide. Greenaway was by the car, bringing out a cardboard box.

Cornwell turned and saw a girl dressed in a blue padded jacket, jeans and boots, her dark hair blown back by the wind. She stood beside a shaggy grey moorland pony that no one would look at twice.

"Not again!" Cornwell groaned. He'd already come across one of these wild ponies in the middle of the night, and that one had put up a terrific fight before the trainer had finally managed to tie him up.

Without warning this pony charged him and knocked him off his feet, sending him sprawling across the ground.

Cornwell swore and stayed down. The pony stood over him, threatening to trample him, while Greenaway dropped the box and ran to the rescue.

Meanwhile Krista dashed inside the barn.

Three horses were tethered in the dark, without food or water. As her eyes grew used to the gloom, Krista made out Night Watchman. The poor creature was filthy. He was tied so close to the wall that he could not turn his head.

"Poor thing!" Krista murmured, rapidly working at the knot to release him.

Outside, North Star's hooves stamped the ground around Cornwell's head. "This thing's crazy! It's going to kill me!"

"Steady!" Krista whispered as she approached the chestnut racehorse.

Lady Madonna shook all over. She looked nothing like the fine creature Krista had seen on TV only last Saturday. Her head hung low, her eyes were dull, her spirit broken by the terrifying events.

So once more Krista worked at the knot which tethered the horse to an iron ring, trying to soothe her. "You're going to be fine," she promised. "We won't let them harm you any more!"

"Get this pony away from me!" Cornwell yelled.

Greenaway ran at North Star, who lunged back at him and bit him on the arm.

Greenaway leaped back, leaving his boss on the ground. "It won't let me near!"

"Get the girl!" Cornwell ordered, once more trying to fend off North Star's hooves.

Krista had released Lady Madonna and at last found Shining Star. He was tethered in a corner, his back legs hobbled with a length of thick rope. She cried out when she saw how they had shackled him.

"Take the others outside before the men come," he told her with what seemed like his last ounce of strength.

Krista obeyed. She turned back to Night Watchman and Lady Madonna, herding them towards the daylight, where she could see Cornwell still lying on the ground, and Greenaway forced back from the doorway. "Go ahead," she urged the terrified horses.

At first they were too spooked to go forward. They tried to turn and retreat into their prison, but Krista grabbed their lead-ropes, one in each hand, and led them on, offering them their freedom.

They resisted. Outside, Greenaway spotted what was happening and ran for the door.

But North Star was too quick for him. He whirled away from Cornwell and put himself between Greenaway and the door, giving

Krista one more chance to lead Lady Madonna and Night Watchman out into the open.

"We won't let them harm you!" she promised again, willing the horses to gallop free.

And at last they seized their chance, breaking away from Krista and running into the field, rearing up and whinnying in terror.

"That's good – run!" Krista said, turning once more to rescue Shining Star.

Meanwhile, Cornwell was back on his feet. He saw the racehorses flee from the barn, galloping down the field towards the manor.

Rage seized him. He ran to his car and seized an iron crowbar from the back, wielding it over his head as he ran towards North Star.

Inside the barn, Krista ran to untie the rope from around Shining Star's legs. "Keep still, I can do this!" she gasped, fumbling and struggling with the knot.

"I knew you would come," he said calmly. "And my brother is strong. He will not let the men enter."

At the door, North Star reared up against Cornwell and Greenaway. His front hooves flailed in the air. He crashed them down, charged at Cornwell and forced him to drop the bar, kicking out at Greenaway with his back legs and catching him on the thigh.

Greenaway grabbed his leg and cried out. "I'm out of here!" he groaned, beginning to hobble away.

Cornwell swore at him. "I won't be beaten by a kid and a pair of wild ponies!" he cried, picking up the bar and running at North Star once more.

"OK, I've untied your legs," Krista told Shining Star. She moved on to the rope which tethered him to the wall. "It won't be long now!"

Shining Star waited patiently. "Such slender fingers," he said. "Such a large heart in a small frame!"

At last Krista freed her magical pony. He took unsteady steps towards the door, looking out at the horses running free and his brother keeping Cornwell and Greenaway at bay. "All will be well," he promised.

And as he spoke the words, Krista saw a

white Land Rover with a flashing blue light driving fast up the hill towards them.

The two men saw the police car too. Greenaway yelled a warning to his boss, who began to run towards his car.

North Star went to stand beside Shining Star and Krista. All three watched as three men jumped out of the police Land Rover. They pounced on Cornwell and Greenaway, there was a struggle then the policemen pinned the two criminals to the ground.

"Thank heavens!" Krista gasped, trembling with relief.

"My brother, I am glad to see you," Shining Star said in a low voice. "And Krista, I thank you from the bottom of my heart."

Chapter Nine

The arrests were made and Cornwell and Greenaway were shoved into the back of the police Land Rover. Then a figure came running across the fields from Westgate Manor.

"It's Georgie!" Krista watched the stable girl climb a wall and cautiously approach Lady Madonna, who had come to a halt as soon as she had seen her.

A policeman came up to Krista and her two ponies. "You were taking a big risk there," he told her. "What would have happened if we hadn't shown up?"

"I would have been OK," she replied. "North Star would have looked after me. Anyway, we set the horses free, didn't we?"

The policeman nodded.

"Cornwell was planning to put them down," she explained. "We had to do something!"

"The sensible thing would have been to ring us, like Georgie did."

"It would have been too late," Krista pointed out. She gave a puzzled frown. "Anyway, how come she did that?"

"It seems Georgie suspected her boss all along. The more she thought about it, the more his version of events didn't seem to fit the facts. In the end she gave us a call."

"When?" Krista saw in the distance that

Georgie had taken hold of Madonna's lead-rope and gently calmed her down. Then the stable girl walked up to Night Watchman and did the same.

"About an hour ago. She finally plucked up the courage to tell us her doubts. We got on to it straight away." The policeman nodded to one of his fellow officers who was gesturing for him to get in the car. "To tell you the truth, we were already keeping a close eye on Cornwell. This arrest doesn't come as any surprise."

"I hate him!" Krista muttered. "He would have killed two incredible horses!"

The policeman nodded, setting off towards the Land Rover. "Don't worry, there won't be

any animals for him to mistreat where he's going! He'll be locked up in prison for a very long time."

As the police car drew away with the prisoners, Krista, North Star and Shining Star made their way down the hill and Georgie strode up to meet them.

"Is everyone OK?" the stable girl asked.

Krista nodded. "Where are Night Watchman and Lady Madonna?"

"I handed them over to one of the other grooms. We think they should be OK once we've treated Night Watchman's cuts, bedded them both down and fed them." She beamed at Krista. "Hey, you have a knack of showing up at odd times – and thank heavens you do!"

Krista blushed. "What'll happen now?"

"Well, with Cornwell in prison, they'll have to find a new trainer for the yard." Georgie shrugged. "I guess it'll be up to the owners."

"And will you stay?"

"I reckon so." Georgie smiled. "Now that my precious Madonna's back, how can I leave?"

"Cool!" Krista was pleased with the news, and glad for the two racehorses that Georgie would be there to look after them.

"Hey, come down to the stable and check the horses," Georgie urged. She reached out to stroke Shining Star, who nuzzled her palm. "Cute!" she grinned.

"Thanks for the offer, but we have to go," Krista gabbled. "I've got to get back home for a Christmas concert."

She didn't tell Georgie that "home" was hundreds of miles away, or that she would be flying there with her two magical ponies!

Shining Star and North Star stood with Krista on the brow of the hill, watching the relieved stable girl make her way back to the yard.

North Star looked up at the grey sky, watching small snowflakes begin to whirl in the wind. "Are you strong enough to fly to Galishe?" he asked Shining Star.

His brother nodded. "I feel my strength return now that all has ended happily. But first, Krista, climb up and let us take you home."

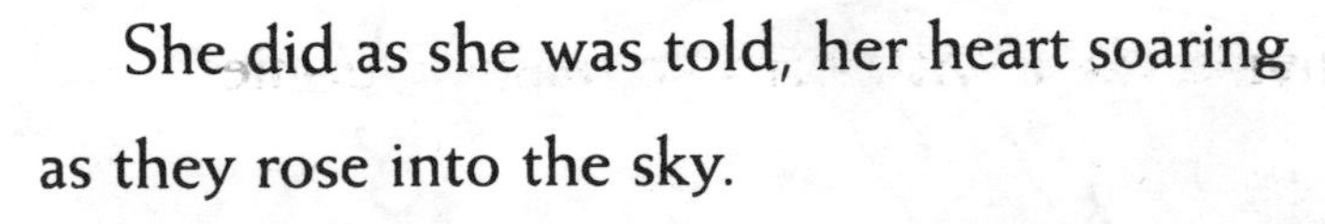

She did as she was told, her heart soaring as they rose into the sky.

They flew over Westgate Manor and saw Georgie taking buckets of feed to Madonna and Night Watchman, back in their stables where they belonged. They flew over the town with its market place, church and police station.

Then Shining Star followed North Star high into the sky, trailing silver mist, entering

the bright, whirling tunnel that would take Krista home to Whitton, to Christmas and to the brilliant day-after-Boxing-Day Arncliff ride!